Reading +
language

Published by Scholastic Inc., 90 Old Sherman Turnpike, Danbury, CT 06816.

SCHOLASTIC and associated logos are trademarks and/or registered trademarks of Scholastic Inc.

ISBN 0-439-90707-1

Printed in the U.S.A.

First Scholastic Printing, February 2007

The Traveler's Tale

by
Erica David

illustrated by
Dave Aikins

SCHOLASTIC INC.

New York   Toronto   London   Auckland   Sydney
Mexico City   New Delhi   Hong Kong   Buenos Aires

"It's a beautiful day for a story," Storyteller Tyrone observed, as he looked out across the sand dunes of the Great Desert. "And when I tell the world's most exciting story at the Arabian All-Star Talent Show at the Oasis, I'm sure to win first place!"

And so Storyteller Tyrone began his trek across the desert.

After a while, Storyteller Tyrone's path led him into a grove of palm trees. A few steps in, he heard a strange noise. Tyrone looked up and saw that the trees were moving their branches to block his way. Soon he was walled in by branches, and the path had disappeared!

"Hey! Let me through!" Storyteller Tyrone cried. "I have a talent show to get to!"

Just then a stranger stepped through the trees, playing a beautiful melody on a flute. At the sound of the music, the palm trees began to sway, lifting their branches out of Tyrone's way and letting him pass.

"How'd you do that?" asked Tyrone.

"Those trees are no match for my magic flute. I'm Uniqua the Tree Charmer."

"Well, thank you, Tree Charmer Uniqua. You got here just in time," Tyrone said. "I'm on my way to the Arabian All-Star Talent Show to tell the most exciting story in the world. Would you like to come with me?"

"Sure!" Uniqua answered eagerly.

Tyrone and Uniqua walked and walked. Soon a fierce wind began to blow. Sand swirled all around them.

"Uh-oh, it's a sandstorm!" Uniqua exclaimed.

"Run!" Tyrone cried.

But it was too late. Tyrone and Uniqua were swept up into the storm.

Suddenly a powerful stranger arrived. He lifted his staff and called out to the wind, "O Mighty Storm, release these travelers!"

As soon as the stranger spoke, the winds died down and the storm stopped.

"Wow!" said Uniqua. "Where'd you learn to do that?"

"It's an old family secret. I'm Pablo, Master of Storms."

"Nice to meet you, Master Pablo," said Tyrone.
"We're on our way to the Arabian All-Star Talent Show
at the Oasis."

"The Oasis? I love seeing shows there!" Pablo replied.
"May I come with you?"

"Of course," said Tyrone.

The three travelers continued their journey. Before long, they came to an old bridge at the edge of a cliff.

"This bridge looks kind of rickety," Uniqua said.
"Do you think we can make it across?" asked Pablo.

"We have to," Tyrone answered. "That sandstorm made us late for the talent show. This is the quickest way to the Oasis."

Uniqua and Pablo followed Tyrone across the shaky bridge. It creaked and twisted beneath their feet.

"We're almost there!" Tyrone called. He had just stepped over a missing plank when the ropes broke and the boards fell from under their feet!

"Oh no!" Uniqua cried, as the three travelers tumbled through the air.

"I'm coming, oh travelers!" called a voice. Out of the clear blue sky, a stranger appeared flying on a magic carpet.

The stranger caught Tyrone, Uniqua, and Pablo on
his carpet.

"Thank you for saving us!" Pablo exclaimed.

"All in a day's work. I'm Austin, Carpet Pilot, first class."

"Say, Carpet Pilot Austin, do you think you could give us a ride to the Oasis?" Uniqua asked.

"We're late for the Arabian All-Star Talent Show," added Tyrone. "I have to get there in time to tell the world's most exciting story."

"Sure," Austin replied. "I've always wanted to see the Arabian All-Star Talent Show."

The four travelers arrived at the Oasis just as the last performer left the stage.

"Let's have a round of applause for our last contestant!" said Host Tasha. "Now it's time to pick our winner!"

"Wait! Wait!" cried Tyrone, as he and his friends rushed

onto the stage. "I'm Storyteller Tyrone and I'm sorry I'm late. But you won't believe what happened to me on the way to the show."

"Okay, well, let's hear it," Host Tasha said.

"As I set out across the Great Desert, some enchanted palm trees blocked my path," Tyrone told the audience. "I was trapped and couldn't find my way out!"

"But I charmed the trees with my magic flute to clear the way," Uniqua explained.

"Then we got caught in a fierce sandstorm. The wind lifted us right off the ground!" said Tyrone.

"But I used my magic to stop the storm," Pablo added.

"Then we had to cross a canyon on an old, rickety bridge. But when we got halfway across, it collapsed; and we fell through the air!" Tyrone said.

"But I caught them in the nick of time and gave them a ride to the show on my magic carpet," Austin chimed in.

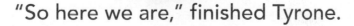

"So here we are," finished Tyrone.

"Wow, that's the most exciting story I've ever heard!"
Host Tasha exclaimed. "What do you say, audience? Have
we found our winners?"

The audience jumped to its feet and cheered.

"It's official," announced Host Tasha. "I hereby award
you all first prize."

Storyteller Tyrone turned to his new friends. "I can't wait to see what happens to us on our way home!" he said with a grin.

Nick Jr. Play-to-Learn™ Fundamentals
Skills every child needs, in stories every child will love!

colors + shapes	Recognizing and identifying basic shapes and colors in the context of a story.	
emotions	Learning to identify and understand a wide range of emotions, such as happy, sad, and excited.	
imagination	Fostering creative thinking skills through role-play and make-believe.	
math	Recognizing early math in the world around us, such as patterns, shapes, numbers, and sequences.	
music + movement	Celebrating the sounds and rhythms of music and dance.	
physical	Building coordination and confidence through physical activity and play.	
problem solving	Using critical thinking skills, such as observing, listening, and following directions, to make predictions and solve problems.	
reading + language	Developing a lifelong love of reading through high interest stories and characters.	
science	Fostering curiosity and an interest in the natural world around us.	
social skills + cultural diversity	Developing respect for others as unique, interesting people.	

Conversation Spark

Questions and activities for play-to-learn parenting.

Tyrone told an exciting story in the talent show. What would you do in a talent show?